THE HUNGER HEROES

Snack Cabinet Sabotage

BY JARRETT LERNER

Aladdin

NEW YORK LONDON TORONTO SYDNEY NEW DELHI

In a seemingly ordinary city...

Atop a seemingly ordinary building...

Live a group of EXTRAordinary heroes...

ALADDIN / An imprint of Simon & Schuster Children's Publishing Division / 1230 Avenue of the Americas, New York, New York 10020 / First Aladdin edition August 2022 / Copyright © 2022 by Jarrett Lerner / All rights reserved, including the right of reproduction in whole or in part in any form. / ALADDIN and related logo are registered trademarks of Simon & Schuster, Inc. / For information about special discounts for bulk purchases, please contact Simon & Schuster Special Sales at 1-866-506-1949 or business@simonandschuster.com. / The Simon & Schuster Speakers Bureau can bring authors to your live event. For more information or to book an event contact the Simon & Schuster Speakers Bureau at 1-866-248-3049 or visit our website at www.simonspeakers.com. / Series designed by Jarrett Lerner & Karin Paprocki / Book designed by Jarrett Lerner & Alicia Mikles / The illustrations for this book were rendered digitally. / The text of this book was hand-lettered. / Manufactured in China 0522 SCP / 10 9 8 7 6 5 4 3 2 1 / Library of Congress Control Number 2021945987 / ISBN 9781534480353 (hc) / ISBN 9781534480346 (pbk) / ISBN 9781534480360 (ebook)

For Karen Nagel

THE HUNGER HEROES

MR. TOOTS!

CHiP NiNJA!

TAMMY!

Leonard...?

Oh no. Not THIS again.

Wait! I'm here! I'm right here!

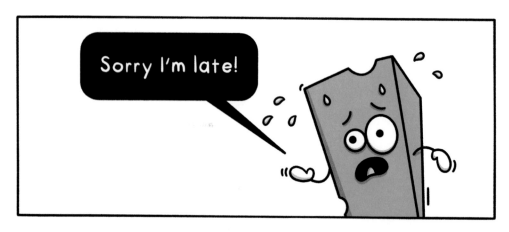

What about Chapter 6? When we—

This panel contains spoilers and has been removed for your own good.

Yes, but, Leonard, if I may point out—

SPROING!

9

CHAPTER 1

It was the end of a long, quiet day at Hunger Heroes headquarters.

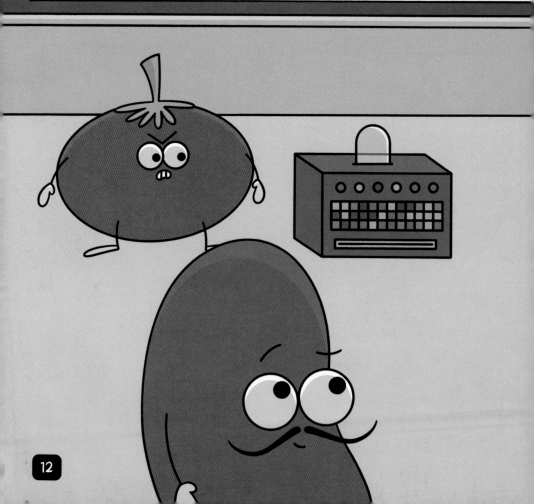

There had been no reports of hungry
kids in the city. There had been no mad
dashes to the Hovercraft. There had
been no flights through the sky and no
heroics on the ground.

What a waste of a perfectly good day.

I, for one, thought it was lovely.

YAWN!

zzzzz

14

It wasn't ALL bad. We got a chance to catch up with old friends.

I guess it was pretty nice to see Carl and Bonnie and Ava.

15

Slow down, friends. Take it easy. Ava's a fan, that's all. She's one of many who want to know everything there is to know about the Hunger—

It was an alert! The rest of the heroes gathered around Tammy as the report finished printing. Even Leonard joined, though he was far from happy about it.

20

Leonard's question hung in the air, unanswered.

Tammy passed the report to Mr. Toots for a closer look.

10-52

Snackless Babysitter

NAME: Gabby

LOCATION: Richardson residence

LAST MEAL: Peanut butter banana sandwich; two pickle spears; 11:45 a.m.

ADDITIONAL INFO: Prone to bouts of hanger

She's a good kid. She volunteers at the food bank, and helps coach her brother's soccer team. She just...gets hangry now and then.

I've got a question: Who DOESN'T get hangry now and then?

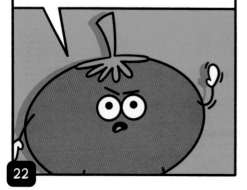

I've got a question too....

WHAT KIND OF A PERSON WOULD LEAVE A BABYSITTER IN A HOUSE WITH NO SNACKS?!

Something about it does feel a little...off. We've never gotten a 10-52 from the Richardsons before....

What are you saying, Chip?

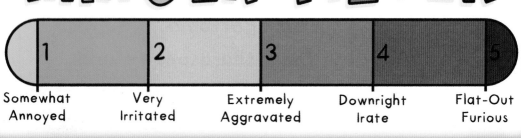

CHAPTER 2

As they soared toward the Richardsons' house, the Hunger Heroes discussed strategy.

27

What do you mean?

I mean that this seems like a pretty simple operation.

Land the Hovercraft on the chimney....

Parachute down it....

Feed the kid.

Piece of cake.

And what do you all have against KNOCKING ON THE FRONT DOOR?!
ALERT! ALERT! ALERT! ALERT! ALERT! ALERT! ALERT!
ALERT!
ALERT! ALERT! ALERT! ALERT!
Friends, we may not even make it to the Richardsons'....

Chip Ninja scanned the Hovercraft's many flashing monitors, then delivered the bad news: "It's telling us that something's wrong with our landing gear."

It wasn't her best landing—but Tammy did it!

CHAPTER 2½

Inside the Richardsons' house, Gabby had just put the baby to bed.

HANGER METER

1	2	3	4	5

Somewhat Annoyed   Very Irritated   Extremely Aggravated   Downright Irate   Flat-Out Furious

CHAPTER 3

The Hunger Heroes quickly cleaned themselves up and climbed out of the bush where they had crash-landed.

43

Okay, well, why are there a bunch of dog treats on the lawn?

It IS a bit odd....

First our landing gear malfunctions....

And now this.

I'm sure there's a reasonable explanation. Perhaps someone accidentally spilled their bag of treats.

CHAPTER 4

The Hunger Heroes had no clue what to do. Fear had them frozen in place!

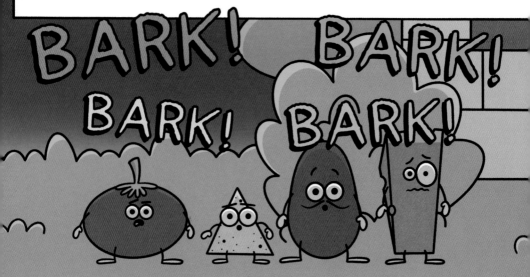

Not so fast, Leonard. We just have to get to the front door—

before the dogs get to us!

But the crew hadn't made it more than a few feet before the pack of hungry pups charged onto the Richardsons' lawn, quickly blocking the Heroes' path to safety.

BARK! BARK! BARK! BARK!

You know, I always thought it would be an especially wild ride in the Hovercraft that finally did me in, but I guess I was wrong. I guess I go out in a blur of slobber and fangs.

51

CRISS-
CROSS

TARTAR SAUCE!

As soon as the words left Tammy's and Chip Ninja's lips, the Hunger Heroes exploded into action.

Each of them darted in a different direction, causing the dogs to chase after them, twisting and turning in chaotic, confusing, dizzying loops.

Tammy could have happily gone on Crisscrossing and Tartar Saucing for the rest of the night. But when she happened past a skateboard on the lawn, she skidded to a stop.

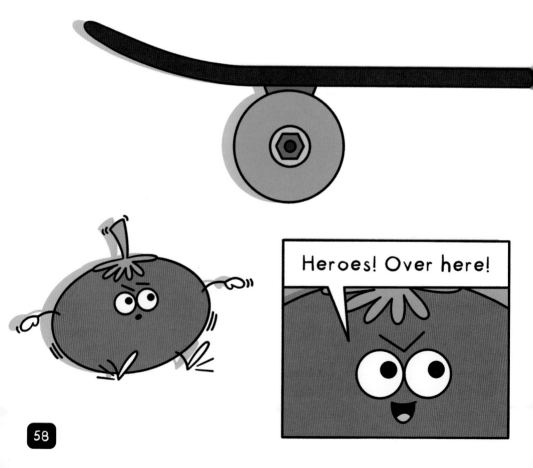

Heroes! Over here!

The Heroes didn't hesitate. But once they were atop the board, Leonard couldn't help but ask, "WHAT ARE WE DOING ON THIS THING?!"

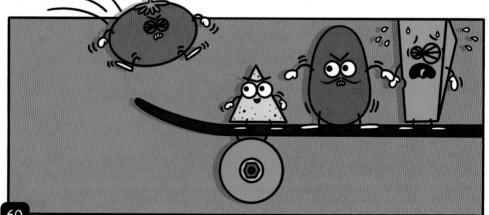

For a terrifying moment, the Hunger Heroes hung there, high up in the air...

and then they came crashing down.

65

CHAPTER 4½

Inside the Richardsons' house, the situation had gone from bad to worse. The baby was awake—and WAILING.

WAA-WAAAHHHHHH!

Gabby doubted she had the patience to soothe a baby with her stomach as empty as it was.

But she'd searched the entire house for snacks...

JUNK DRAWER

CRAFT BOX

LAUNDRY ROOM

BATHROOM

and she hadn't found a single crumb.

As the baby's cries grew louder, Gabby did everything she could to fight off the hanger.

But it was no use.

CHAPTER 5

Back outside, on the Richardsons'
roof, the Hunger Heroes were gazing
up at the chimney.

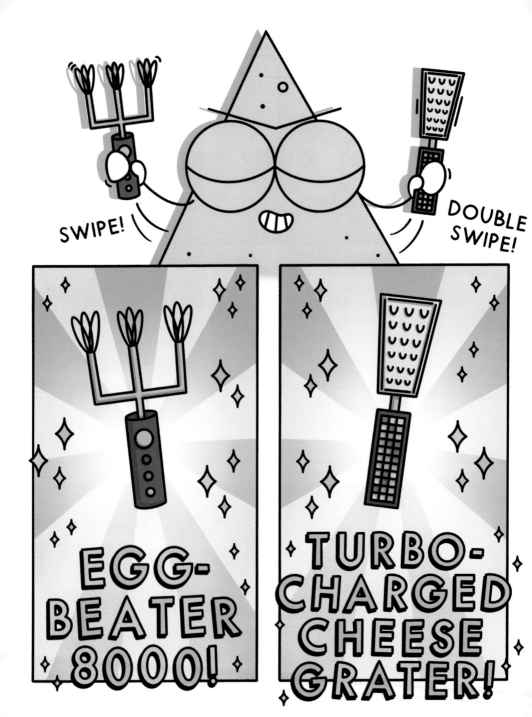

73

This should do the trick.

All right, Heroes. Let's do this.

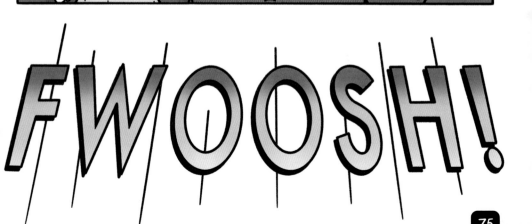

So, ah—I've actually never used this thing before.

But I think all you have to do is press this butt—

FWOOSH!

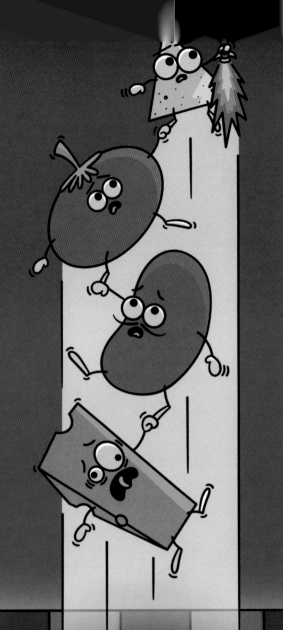

Within seconds, the Heroes had flown dozens of feet up in the air.

Tammy shouted to Chip Ninja: "Don't take us TOO high. Quick! Press the other button!"

Leonard! Aim us toward the chimney!

I don't wanna! I don't wanna!

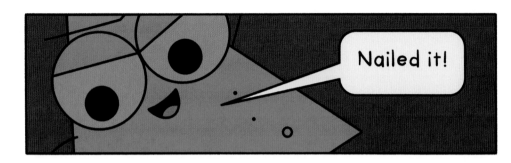

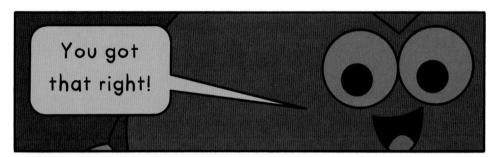

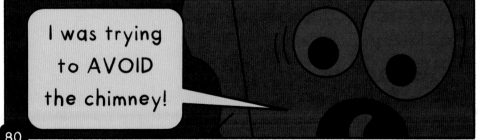

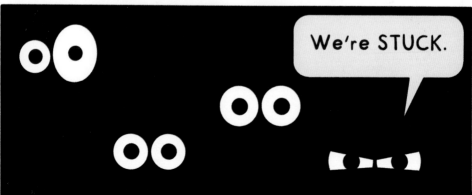

CHAPTER 6

Throughout their superheroic history together, the Hunger Heroes had found themselves in many tight spots.

But never had the crew found themselves in THIS tight of a spot— not to mention this DARK of a spot.

They were trapped in the Richardsons' chimney!

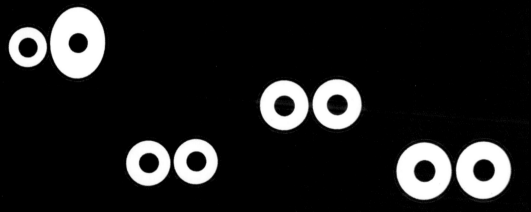

83

85

Oh, wait. Now I smell it.

SNIFF! SNIFF!

Definitely guacamole.

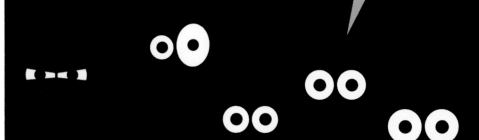

Can we please stop it with the guacamole?! Gabby is down there, hangry, with a crying baby! We need to figure out how to get out of—

I mean, what kind of people would leave a babysitter without any snacks?

I'd just like to point out that I've been asking that question since Chapter 1.

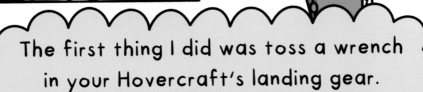

The first thing I did was toss a wrench in your Hovercraft's landing gear.

TOSS!

Then I came here. I ate some of the Richardsons' snacks and hid all the rest.

But...Ava. We saw you this morning. You were perfectly good.

How did you go bad so quickly? And why?!

Why? WHY?! To prove, once and for all, that you so-called HEROES aren't even half as great as you think you are. I mean, you four think you're soooooooo cool.

Living on top of a big, fancy building...
Flying around town in your supercool Hovercraft.

creeeak

Wait a minute....
Did I just say "cool"?

I did NOT mean
that. I...I meant...

CREEEEEAK

UNcool. Yep. That's what I meant to—

CREAK
CREAK
CREAK
CREAK
CREAK

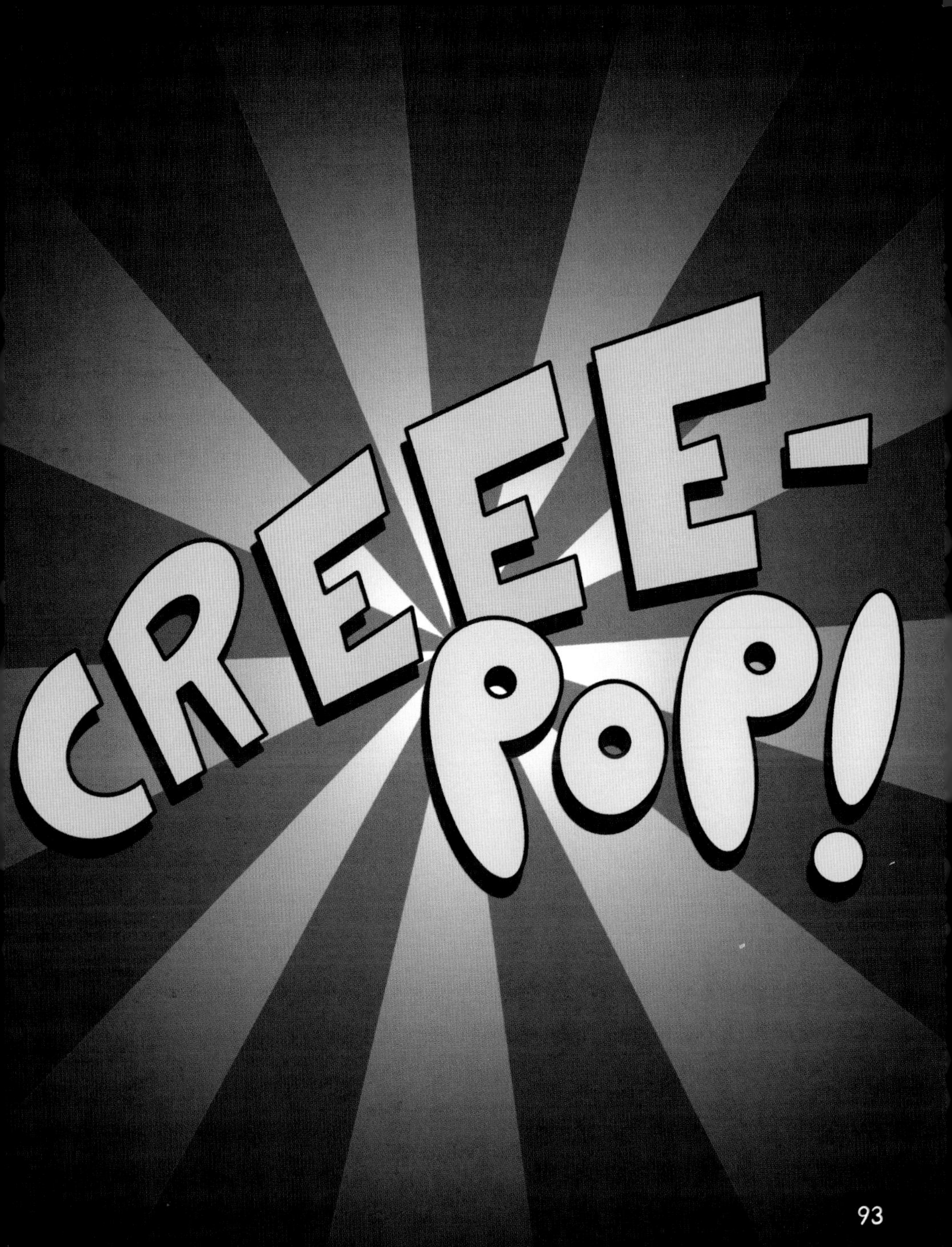
CREEE-POP!

It wasn't the most graceful entrance....

But the Hunger Heroes had finally made it into the Richardsons' house!

The mission, however, was far from complete. In fact, it looked like the difficulties were only beginning....

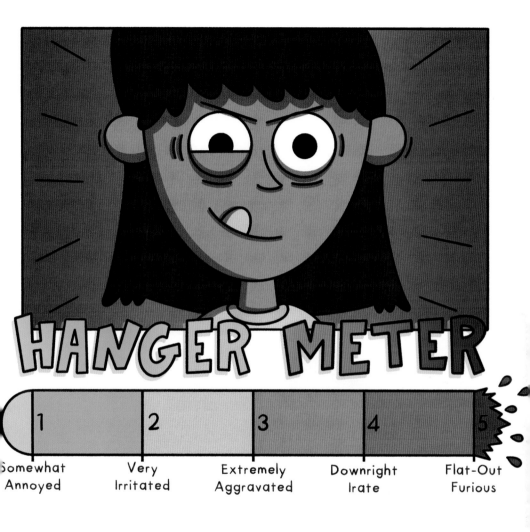

HANGER METER

1	2	3	4	5
Somewhat Annoyed	Very Irritated	Extremely Aggravated	Downright Irate	Flat-Out Furious

Gabby was hangrier than ever. She looked at the Hunger Heroes and Ava like THEY might make the perfect snack!

CHAPTER 7

As the Richardson baby's cries grew louder and more desperate, Gabby closed the distance between herself and the superheroic taco ingredients.

102

Mr. Toots took a step toward Ava. "Are you here to sabotage us," he asked the avocado, "or CELEBRATE us?"

But before she could answer, Tammy said, "I'll tell you what I'M here to do."

Chip Ninja—get the Emergency Snack!

Now give me the alley-oop!

Did the tomato just say "alley-poop"?

Is that, like, a poop you find in an alley?

106

The pretzel did the trick! The worst of Gabby's hanger vanished just as soon as the snack reached her stomach.

Her body relaxed. Her eyes refocused.

The baby!

Oh, and sorry about almost eating you back there!

Mr. Toots turned to Ava next. But for one of the first times in the big bean's life, he wasn't sure what to say.

"Don't worry," Ava told him. "I've got something I need to say."

But I think it probably needs its own chapter.

CHAPTER 8

Ava took a moment to collect her thoughts. Then she said:

Ava cleared her throat, then took a deep breath.

"In fact," she told the Heroes, "you could probably say that I'm..."

"Your Number One Fan."

POSTERS

COMIC BOOKS

FAN ART

ACTION FIGURES

"And when I wasn't doing that," Ava continued, "I was dreaming about joining you, in one way or another."

And when I couldn't join you all...

...I got frustrated. And then jealous.

Just then, Gabby stepped back into the room, the baby squirming in her arms.

"It sounds a bit like me," she told Ava.

Once the laughter died down, Ava said, "I happen to know where a cabinet's worth of snacks is stashed!"

Gabby set the baby down and went to let Ava out the door.

"All's well that ends well," Mr. Toots said as Tammy and Chip Ninja followed him to the kitchen.

Keeeeese!

CHAPTER 8½

Ava returned a few minutes after she'd left, a bundle of snacks in tow. While she passed out the food, she told the Hunger Heroes that she'd also removed the wrench from their Hovercraft's landing gear.

"Shouldn't give you any more trouble," the avocado said.

You're a good egg, Ava. You really are.

121

With the baby once more asleep and Gabby's hanger vanquished, it was time for Ava and the Hunger Heroes to leave.

123

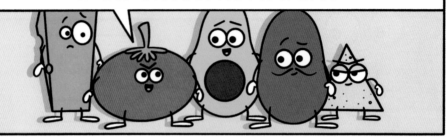

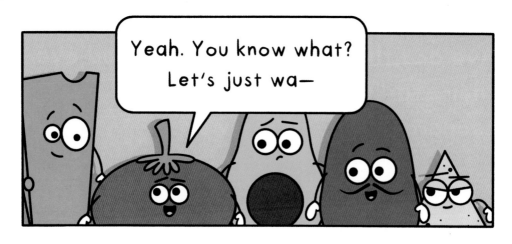

BARK! BARK!
BARK! BARK! BARK!
BARK! BARK!

Ava and the Hunger Heroes soared over their starlit city. Everyone—even Leonard—enjoyed the view.